For Ise and Liv

This edition published by Kids Can Press in 2020

Originally published by Uitgeverij Hoogland & Van Klaveren in Hoorn, the Netherlands, under the title
Kleine wijze wolf
Text © 2017 Gijs van der Hammen
Illustrations © 2017 Hanneke Siemensma
English translation © 2018, 2020 by Laura Watkinson
North American English edition © 2020 Kids Can Press

Translation rights arranged by élami agency

Kids Can Press gratefully acknowledges the financial support of the Government of Ontario, through Ontario Creates.

Published in Canada and the U.S. by Kids Can Press Ltd.
25 Dockside Drive, Toronto, ON M5A 0B5

Kids Can Press is a Corus Entertainment Inc. company

www.kidscanpress.com

Printed and bound in Buji, Shenzhen, China, in 3/2020 by WKT Company

CM 20 0 9 8 7 6 5 4 3 2 1

Library and Archives Canada Cataloguing in Publication

Title: Little wise wolf / written by Gijs van der Hammen ; illustrated by Hanneke Siemensma.
Other titles: Kleine wijze wolf. English
Names: Hammen, Gijs van der, author. | Siemensma, Hanneke, illustrator. | Watkinson, Laura, translator.
Description: Previously published: Bristol: Book Island, 2018. | Translation of: Kleine wijze wolf. | Translated from Dutch by Laura Watkinson.
Identifiers: Canadiana 20200178970 | ISBN 9781525305498 (hardcover)
Classification: LCC PT5882.18.A46 K5413 2020 | DDC j839.313/7 — dc23

This publication has been made possible with financial support from the Dutch Foundation for Literature.

Nederlands
letterenfonds
dutch foundation
for literature

Little Wise Wolf

Gijs van der Hammen   •   Hanneke Siemensma

Translated by Laura Watkinson

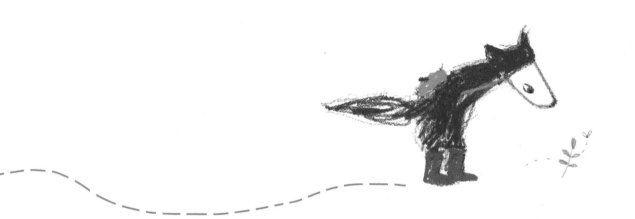

KIDS CAN PRESS

Far away, on the other side of the mountains, there lived a little wolf. He read big books. He discovered new stars. He knew every herb. He knew everything! Because he knew so much, almost everyone called him Little Wise Wolf. And that made him feel rather proud.

The animals who lived nearby often went to see him with difficult questions.

"Little Wise Wolf!" called the bear. "What do butterflies eat?"

"Little Wise Wolf, where does the rain come from?" asked the goat.

"Little Wise Wolf, how many stars are in the sky?" barked the badger.

"Wise Wolf, I can't read!" squeaked a small rabbit. "Will you help me?"

But Little Wise Wolf did not want to be disturbed. He still had so many big books to read so that he could become even wiser.

"I don't have time for your questions," he muttered.

His door remained closed.

One day, he heard a tapping at his window. A big, black bird flew into his house. It was the king's crow, with a note around his neck.

Dear Wise Wolf,
I am very ill. Only you can make me better.
Please help!
Yours,
The king

"No time!" shouted Little Wise Wolf. "There's a plant I need to research. And a big book to finish reading. And I think I've just found a new star. I'm really rather busy right now."

"When the king calls, you have to come," said the crow.

Butterflies

GRIMM

The Universe

ATLAS

PLATO

Little Wise Wolf thought long and hard, as he liked to do. Then he packed everything he needed. The next morning, he set off.

"Little Wise Wolf," said the mouse, "where are you going?"

"I'm off to see the king. I don't have time for your questions," he growled. And he cycled away.

"I've heard that the king is ill," said the badger, "and only the wolf can make him better."

"Hmm," said the bear. "But it's such a long way to the castle. Do you think he needs our help?"

The road was very long.

Little Wise Wolf pedaled and pedaled and pedaled.

The road went up and the road went down.
Little Wise Wolf walked and walked and walked.

The mountains rose higher and higher.

Little Wise Wolf climbed and climbed and climbed.

"He's going so slowly," whispered the goat. "Do you think he needs our help?"

"Well, we're really rather busy right now," said the rabbits.

Around midday, it started to rain. Big drops fell from the sky.

"That little wolf is getting soaked," said the frog. "Do you think he needs our help?"

Evening fell, and it grew dark. Little Wise Wolf was tired of walking.
"I'm cold. My stomach's rumbling. My feet hurt. And I'm lost. Maybe I'm not as wise as everyone says. I think someone else will have to make the king better."
Then, in the distance, he saw a light.

And there, deep in the forest, Little Wise Wolf found a tent — and a pot of soup simmering on a campfire. He had no idea where they came from, but he had a lovely night's sleep.

"Wake up, Little Wise Wolf!" shouted the bear the next morning. "You have to go and see the king!"
Little Wise Wolf was very surprised.
"Did you all come here to help me?" he asked.
"Of course we did!" cried the animals.

They took him to the edge of the forest.
"Aren't you coming with me?" asked Little Wise Wolf.
"No. You can do it alone from here," said the bear.

But the city was big, and Little Wise Wolf was soon completely lost again.
"Can anyone tell me how to get to the castle?" he asked quietly.
A friendly cat showed him the way.

Finally, Little Wise Wolf arrived at the castle gates. But then he couldn't go any farther.

"I don't think I can do it. Someone else will have to make the king better," he said once again.

But the crow pushed him inside. "Go on! The king is waiting for you!"

"Hello, Wise Wolf," said the king weakly. "Thank you for coming."

"I – I – I'm not as wise as everyone says ..." stuttered the little wolf. But the king wouldn't listen.

"Make me better right away," he said. "I don't have time to be ill."

So Little Wise Wolf made some medicine. It was from an herb that only he knew because it was in a book that only he had read. The king swallowed a spoonful, and before long he was back on his feet again.

"Please," begged the king, "stay here and be my royal doctor. I'll give you the tower room so you can look at the stars. No one will disturb you. You can read big books all day long."

But, for once, Little Wise Wolf did not have to think long and hard.

"I need to go back to my friends on the other side of the mountains," he said. "I still have a lot to learn from them."

Now, Little Wise Wolf is never too busy when the other animals come to see him. No one knows how, but he reads just as many big books as before. And he discovers just as many plants and stars. Maybe even more.